Bright
Summaries.com

The Saturnian Poems

BY PAUL VERLAINE

Written by Sophie Chetrit
Translated by Oliver Brown

The Saturnian Poems

BY PAUL VERLAINE

Shed new light
on your favorite books
with

Bright
Summaries.com

www.BrightSummaries.com

PAUL VERLAINE — 5

French poet — 5

THE SATURNIAN POEMS — 7

Verlaine's first collection of poetry — 7

SUMMARY — 9

The opening poem — 9
The Prologue — 9
Melancholia — 9
Etchings — 11
Sad landscapes — 13
Caprices — 14
Other poems — 15
Epilogue — 16

LIGHTING — 17

On the influence of the Parnassians… — 17
… To that of the romantics — 18
The influence of Charles Baudelaire — 20

KEYS TO READING — 22

The poetic form: inversion of the classical
sonnet and odd-numbered lines — 22
The main themes of the collection — 24
Verlaine: symbolist poet — 28

AVENUES FOR REFLECTION — 30

A few questions for further reflection… — 30

TO GO FURTHER — 31

Reference edition — 31
Benchmark studies — 31
Main musical adaptations — 31

PAUL VERLAINE

FRENCH POET

- **Born in 1844 in Metz**
- **Died in 1896 in Paris**
- **Some of his works:**
    - *Fêtes galantes* (1869), a collection of poetry
    - *Romances sans paroles* (1874), collection of poetry
    - *Les poètes maudits* (1884), essay

Born in 1844, Paul Verlaine was a poet of the second half of the 19th century. He was born in Metz in 1844 into a middle-class family and went to Paris to study law. He studied law there and later worked in an insurance company and as an expeditionary at the Paris City Hall. In 1866, he published the *Poèmes Saturniens*. Three years later, his second collection *Fêtes galantes* was published, evoking Watteau's 18th century. He married Mathilde Mauté, a young girl from the Parisian upper middle class, in 1870.

After the siege of Paris and the Paris Commune uprising in 1871, Verlaine, who had met Arthur Rimbaud, left his wife to follow him to England and then to Belgium. During his travels, he wrote a new collection, *Romances sans paroles*. The two poets had a passionate relationship until the famous evening of July 1873, when Verlaine shot his lover and was sentenced to two years in prison, which he served in Brussels and Mons. He then converted to Catholicism and on his release from prison in 1875, he went back to England for a while where he became a teacher, only to return to the Ardennes, to Rethel, where he became friends with one of his pupils, Lucien Létinois, who died in 1883.

The following year, Verlaine published *Les poètes maudits*, a book in which three poets were honoured: Tristan Corbière, Arthur Rimbaud and Stéphane Mallarmé. His fame grew and he was proclaimed the "Prince of Poets", even though he became worn out and led a debauched life until his death from lung congestion in 1896.

THE SATURNIAN POEMS

VERLAINE'S FIRST COLLECTION OF POETRY

- **Genre:** poetry

- **Reference edition:** VERLAINE P., *Poèmes Saturniens*, Gallimard, coll. "Folio", 2010, 96 p.

- **Themes:** time, love, melancholy, music, poetry

Paul Verlaine published the *Poèmes saturniens* at the age of twenty-two, although he is said to have begun writing them while still in high school, at the age of sixteen. He had first thought of calling this collection *Poèmes et Sonnets*, before deciding on the name we know today, in reference to the Roman god and the dark and melancholic planet. Edited on a self-publishing basis and published in 1866 by Alphonse Lemerre, the *Poèmes saturniens* is Paul Verlaine's first collection of poetry in verse. However, this work had only a limited reception, not being considered at the time as a major literary event.

During this period, Verlaine frequented Parisian literary circles and contributed to the first Parnasse contemporain (1866), a collective collection of poems that was the manifesto and illustration of the Parnasse movement. This was a movement in opposition to the Romantic outpourings, which promoted modern poetic art based on formal perfection and impersonal lyricism. His masters, Leconte de Lisle, Baudelaire and Théodore de Banville, had a strong influence on Verlaine's poetry.

Little is known about the genesis of this collection, but the *Saturnian Poems*, like Les *Fleurs du mal* (1857) before them, are based on explicit architecture. They begin with an introductory poem that explains the title, as well as a prologue. Then there are twenty-five poems in four sections: "Melancholia", « Eaux fortes », « Paysages tristes » and « Caprices », plus a dozen free poems followed by an Epilogue that closes the collection. Like the great ancient poets, Verlaine placed his collection under the protection of a god and dedicated the first poem to him. The first poem is dedicated to Saturn, a god who refers to the ineluctable nature of the passing of time.

SUMMARY

THE OPENING POEM

The work opens with an introductory poem in which Verlaine claims the particularity of his poetic project and explains the title of his collection. He contrasts the 'Wise Men of old', the traditional poets, with 'those who were born under the sign of Saturn' (v. 8), whom he later calls the cursed poets. These poets are plagued by melancholy, a melancholy that presents itself both as suffering and as inspiration.

THE PROLOGUE

This introductory poem is followed by a prologue, in which Verlaine takes up a motif already present in the Romantics: that of the poet coexisting among men, but placed on the margins. He explains the place he considers to be his within society.

MELANCHOLIA

Dedicated to the violinist and poet Ernest Boutier, this part was certainly inspired by the engraving *Melancholia* by Albrecht Dürer (German draughtsman, painter and engraver, 1471-1528). It consists of eight sonnets written in alexandrines: 'Resignation', 'Nevermore', 'After three years', 'Vow', 'Lassitude', 'My familiar dream', 'To a woman' and 'Anguish'.

Here, we find memories of lost or idealized loves, in which regret and anguish are central. This section was probably written when Verlaine fell in love with his adopted sister, who rejected his love.

- "Resignation' evokes the rejection of the folly of youth.

- "Nevermore' refers to an idealised past and the nostalgia it evokes despite the chastity of the love described.

- In 'Après trois ans', Verlaine recounts his return to the place of his amorous encounters, using nature to represent his feelings: 'Roses as before, throb, as before' (v. 9).

- In 'Vow', he misses his first loves, loves that are both imaginary and idealised. The fifth poem, 'Lassitude', addresses the question of both the desire for a quiet love and the wear and tear of that same desire.

- "My Familiar Dream' is certainly one of the most famous poems in the collection. It reveals Verlaine's dream of an ideal woman, as well as the many sensations he experiences when in contact with her.

- In 'À une femme', he writes to this ideal woman, exaggerating his suffering and appealing to her compassion. This section ends with 'Anguish', a poem in which Verlaine rejects nature as well as art and religion, themes that usually inspire poets.

While 'Resignation' is an inverted sonnet, consisting of two tercets followed by two quatrains, and 'Lassitude' is an irregular sonnet where the rhymes are kissed and then crossed in the tercets (CCDEED), the other poems are French sonnets following a classical pattern, with many rich rhymes.

ETCHINGS

Dedicated to the nineteenth-century French poet, playwright and novelist François Coppée (1842-1908), the 'Eaux-fortes' section has a title that certainly refers to the etching process using an acid-bitten plate. It includes five poems: 'Croquis parisien', 'Cauchemar', 'Marine', 'Effet de nuit' and 'Grotesques'.

In this part, Verlaine describes a city between desolation and modernity, to which he superimposes dreamy landscapes.

- "Parisian Sketch" offers a bleak description of Paris.

- "Nightmare' takes us into a fantasy world where a rider is swept away in a violent movement.

- In 'Marine', the poet borrows a theme from the Romantics by describing an ocean in a storm, to transpose his existential vertigo.

- « Effet de nuit' then presents us with a disturbing night scene, to which Verlaine gives a pictorial aspect.

- « Grotesques' is a caricature of marginal characters: it describes vagrants and the rejection they suffer.

The poems presented here are very diverse. Metrically, they range from quadrisyllabic to alexandrine. In terms of form, they are composed of one to ten stanzas, which are themselves made up of quatrains as well as quintils, or even fourteen lines in the case of 'Effet de nuit'. Similarly, the rhymes can be crossed (in 'Croquis parisien' and 'Grotesques'), followed (in 'Cauchemar' and 'Effet de nuit') or embraced (in 'Marine'), with both even and odd-numbered lines.

 ## GOOD TO KNOW

The form of the stanzas

A quatrain: is a stanza of four lines.

A quintil: is a stanza of five lines.

A sizain: is a stanza of six lines.

Rhymes

Embraced rhymes: are rhymes framed by other rhymes. They take the form ABBA.

Continuous (or flat) rhymes: are rhymes that follow the AABB pattern.

Cross-rhymes (or alternating rhymes): are constructed in a two-by-two alternation. They follow the ABAB pattern.

Feminine rhymes: a feminine rhyme is when the last phoneme contains a 'caduc e' (e.g. 'O sweet sound of rain', Verlaine)

Masculine rhymes: a masculine rhyme occurs when identical sounds are found at the end of two or more lines ending in a full syllable.

Rich rhymes: are rhymes with three homophonies between tonic vowels and consonants.

Poor rhymes: are characterised by the rhyming of a single phoneme, the final tonic vowel of the words.

Sufficient rhymes: corresponds to the repetition of two identical sounds (for example, horse/loyal).

The worms

Even-numbered verse: has an even number of syllables.

Odd verse: has an odd number of syllables.

SAD LANDSCAPES

The term "Sad Landscapes" refers to a pictorial style, notably present in the works of Jean-Baptiste Corot (French painter and engraver). This section is dedicated to Catulle Mendes, founder of the contemporary Parnassus. It consists of seven poems: 'Sunsets', 'Mystical Evening Twilight', 'Sentimental Walk', 'Night of the Classical Walpurgis', 'Autumn Song', 'The Shepherd's Hour' and 'The Nightingale'.

Verlaine develops his own lyricism by describing autumnal landscapes, reminiscent of the sadness of a dark and haunted soul. In the first two poems, the poet describes the spectacle of setting suns inviting reverie, melancholy and anguish. Then the 'Promenade sentimentale' is a funeral walk through a watery landscape, in which Verlaine laments the absence of the loved one.

« La nuit du Walpurgis classique » heralds the fêtes galantes; « Chanson d'automne » allows the poet to evoke his amorous impulses, and to share his emotions through the description of the landscape. « L'heure du berger » (The Shepherd's Hour) again evokes the coming of night, while « le Rossignol » (The Nightingale), a symbol of the song of love, allows him to evoke a love doomed to disappear and the suffering that ensues. We thus find here a unity of tone and setting.

However, this section remains varied in terms of metre and rhyme. Similarly, the poetic forms are diverse: four poems ('Sunsets', 'Mystical Evening Twilight', 'Sentimental Walk', 'The Nightingale') consist of a single stanza, a 'block' of between thirteen and twenty lines, while 'Classical Walpurgis Night' has an architecture of eleven quatrains, 'Autumn Song' four sizains, and 'The Hour of the Bank' three quatrains.

CAPRICES

The « Caprices » refer to 18th-century engravings, especially those of the Spanish painter and engraver Francisco Goya. This section is dedicated to the poet Henry Winter, who collaborated on the first collection of contemporary Parnassus. It consists of five poems: « Femme et chatte », « Jésuitisme », « La chanson des ingénues », « Une grande dame » and « Monsieur Prudhomme ».

The love relationship and women take centre stage here. There is a 'cunt' ('Femme et chatte'), an 'ingénue' ('La chanson des ingénues'), a 'lady', 'queen' and 'courtesan'

('Une grande dame', v. 8), a 'mistress' ('Sérénade', v. 3), etc. « Femme et chatte », « Jésuitisme » and « La chanson des ingénues » take up the Baudelairian theme of the duplicity of women; Verlaine denounces female perversion and cruelty and the sorrow they cause. In 'Une grande dame', he evokes a cold and inaccessible woman, whom he admires as much as he despises. The ambiguity of Verlaine's relationship with women, which is complex and varied, is thus understood. The section ends with 'Monsieur Prudhomme', a satirical poem in which Verlaine portrays a deeply materialistic bourgeois, whom he contrasts with the poets, who are concerned with the arts and letters, but who are condemned to live on the margins of society.

These poems find their unity in their satirical aspect, although the poetic forms proposed are divergent. 'Woman and Pussy' is an irregular sonnet of octosyllables; 'Jesuitism' a poem in sixteen lines; 'The Song of the Ingenues' a poem in eight quatrains; 'A Great Lady' and 'Monsieur Prudhomme' regular sonnets.

OTHER POEMS

Written mainly in alexandrines, the twelve poems that follow take up the major themes of the collection: melancholy, time and wounded love. They are 'Initium', 'Cavitri', 'Sub Urbe', 'Serenade', 'Un dahlia', 'Nevermore', 'Il Bacio', 'Dans les bois', 'Nocturne parisien', 'Marco', 'César Borgia', 'La mort de Philippe II'.

EPILOGUE

The final section offers three poems; this is the Epilogue. It is about poetic art, inspiration, emotion and work. Verlaine returns to formal issues, as well as to Parnassian aesthetics.

LIGHTING

In the middle of the 19th century, when Verlaine began to write, two movements shared the space of poetic expression: Parnassus and Romanticism. Like Baudelaire before him, Verlaine proposed his own synthesis of these influences.

ON THE INFLUENCE OF THE PARNASSIANS...

When Verlaine wrote the *Poèmes saturniens*, he frequented the Parnassian authors, prolix poets who opposed the romantic outpourings and proposed a modern poetic art. They valued "art for art's sake" (Théophile Gautier), whose sole aim was beauty. Thus, he rejects all the subjective and sentimental lyricism of Romanticism and all social or political commitment.

Considered the leader of the Parnassian movement, Leconte de Lisle was the teacher of the young poets of this school. He wrote the *Poèmes antiques* (1852), the *Poèmes barbares* (1862) and the *Poèmes tragiques* (1884), works that allowed him to enter the Académie française in 1887. He set out the following poetic principles:

- Poetry should be impersonal and restrained

- Poetry should focus on the work of form

- Poetry must aim at beauty, for which antiquity provides the absolute canons

Thus he wants to leave the personal theme and return to the pure sources of antiquity, a time when the poet was a worker forging words. As a pessimistic poet, he sees poetry as a refuge from the disenchantment of the world.

At the same time, it is also the influence of Theodore de Bandeville that is notable. A French poet, playwright and literary critic, he is famous for his *Odes funambulesques* and *Les Exilés* (1867). A friend of Victor Hugo and Théophile Gautier, he was also one of the precursors of Parnasse, professing an exclusive love of beauty and the universal clarity of the poetic act. He was both the enemy of the new realist poetry and the enemy of the romantic drifts.

In his *Confessions*, Verlaine states that he wrote the *Poèmes saturniens* at the age of sixteen, while still in high school, at a time when he was under the influence of Leconte de Lisle and his followers. Verlaine's poetry is therefore elaborate, attempting to achieve perfection and rigour in form and in the expression of thought and feeling. He avoids effusiveness, chisels his verse and thus follows the Parnassian precepts. He also uses these precepts as a source of inspiration for his writing. The poem 'Resignation', for example, is inspired by Banville's characteristic taste for the Orient, but also by the rare rhymes that are characteristic of the movement.

... TO THAT OF THE ROMANTICS

Born in Germany at the end of the 18th century, Romanticism appeared in France at the beginning of the 19th century. It was the second cultural movement to come to the fore when Verlaine published his poems. It is a cultural and literary movement, which touched all the arts, opposing the classical tradition and the rationalism of the Enlightenment. It favoured personal expression and gave the artist the opportunity to explore all the possibilities of art in order to express his feelings.

The great themes of Romanticism are melancholy and suffering, nature, dreams, history and political commitment. These major Romantic themes can be found in Verlaine. First of all, melancholy is present in the collection, as the title of the first section 'Melancholia' indicates. The theme of love is also present. "My Familiar Dream', a sonnet written in alexandrines and consisting of two quatrains and two tercets with kissed rhymes; for example, deals with the impossible love for a woman while at the same time seeking a form of musicality. The poet oscillates between the happiness of this love and the suffering it causes since it cannot be achieved. The poem, therefore, has a romantic essence.

Furthermore, it should be noted that Verlaine explicitly draws inspiration from the great Romantic authors, such as François-René de Chateaubriand, Gérard de Nerval and Alfred Musset. In 'Mon rêve familier', for example, he is inspired by the figure of the Sylphide, which Chateaubriand uses in his *Mémoires d'outre-tombe* and in *René*. In 'Monsieur Prudhomme', intertextuality is again visible, particularly through the image of the 'charmille', an image used both in Musset's proverbs and in Nerval's writings when he speaks of love.

However, it is Victor Hugo's texts that are a major source of inspiration. In the 'Ballade des ingénues', for example, there is a reference to the character Caussade, whom he portrays in the play *Marion Delorme*. A famous libertine, he chases after ingenue women and longs for them. In addition to these references, the works of Victor Hugo are also the source of entire poems, such as 'La mort de Philippe II' inspired by the collection of poems *La légende des siècles* (1859). Verlaine appears as a committed poet, although only on rare occasions is he perceived as such. Here, he imagines Philip II, son of Charles V, on his deathbed, regretting that he had encouraged the Inquisition to secure the support of the Pope and establish his rule.

THE INFLUENCE OF CHARLES BAUDELAIRE

Baudelaire was romantic because of his temperament and his admiration for Victor Hugo, to whom he dedicated the «Tableaux Parisiens». He is a Parnassian because of the principles to which he adheres: work, mastery, and rigour. He was aware of both the weaknesses of Romanticism and the limits of Parnassian aesthetic intransigence. It was by proposing a third way that he invented a poetic modernity sheltered from the excesses of both movements. *The Fleurs du mal* (1857) are the illustration of this modernity; they synthesise the two movements while exploring new possibilities of creation and expression.

Baudelaire believes in the imagination as a reasoned faculty of creation; he argues that the imagination is worked and constructed, which makes him a precursor of symbolism. In terms of form, he remained classical, and the use of the sonnet and the alexandrine remained the majority in this work which caused a scandal. He chose to write poetry in which the poet is a victim of spleen, a state of physical, moral and intellectual depression. It is this spleen that allows him to explore new spaces and question his writing.

The Fleurs du mal had a major influence on the poets of the second half of the 19th century, including Verlaine. In the *Poèmes saturniens*, he appropriated Baudelaire's satirical style and his taste for provocation, adopting a style close to his own. This influence is marked in poems such as 'Femme et chatte', where the exclamatory apostrophe 'scélérate' (v. 5) recalls Baudelaire's provocation. Similarly, in 'Monsieur Prudhomme', Verlaine uses the comic register as he satirizes a materialistic bourgeoisie: 'He is a mayor and a family man' (v. 1).

In addition, Baudelaire's own urban theme is apparent in 'Nocturne parisien'. Verlaine also takes up the theme of spleen, particularly in the poem 'Anguish', where negation is very present. However, his writing is very personal, intimate and tinged with solitude. The memories evoked are vague, which gives them a universal dimension.

KEYS TO READING

THE POETIC FORM: INVERSION OF THE CLASSICAL SONNET AND ODD-NUMBERED LINES

Many sonnets are present in Verlaine's work. Of the thirty-nine *Poèmes saturniens*, eleven are sonnets. There are eight in the 'Melancholia' section and three in the 'Caprice' section. These sonnets are framed by a sequence of poems or sections without sonnets. There is thus a strophic alternation.

A sonnet is a poetic form, made popular in the 16th century by the poets of the Pléiade. It came back into fashion in the 19th century by Théophile Gautier, the Parnassians and Charles Baudelaire. Written first in decasyllables and then in alexandrines, its strophic organisation is fixed: it comprises fourteen lines, two quatrains followed by two tercets. The meaning must be complete after each quatrain and each tercet. Similarly, the rhyme scheme is subject to certain constraints. Until the 16th century, the prevailing practice was for the rhymes to be embraced in the quatrains and identical in the two stanzas (ABBA/ABBA). For the tercets, the Italian sonnet proposes the following scheme: CCD EED.

In his *Petit traité sur le Sonnet*, Théodore de Banville describes the form of the French sonnet. He specifies that the first and fourth lines of the quatrains must rhyme together, as well as the second and third lines of the quatrains. He also states that the first and second lines of the first tercet rhyme, when the third line of the first tercet rhymes with the second line of the second tercet. Thus we have a pattern in ABBA ABBA CCD EDE. In addition to the issues of stanzas and rhymes, the sonnet must respect certain constructional modalities.

The sonnet is divided into two blocks which may show a comparison, an opposition, a progression or two distinct themes linked together. They culminate in a punch line, the very last line being a brief and brilliantly formulated conclusion. The sonnet must also, according to Boileau, reject the slightest deviation from the subject, weak lines, superfluous expressions and repetitions. The lines must be precise and accurate, with rich rhymes alternating between masculine and feminine.

In contrast to these sonnets of finished beauty, Verlaine opposes a desire for poetic modernity and proposes irregular sonnets. Some of Verlaine's sonnets do not follow the patterns of stanza, meter and rhyme distribution, thus marking a gradual abandonment of the imposed rules.

- There are inverted sonnets such as the poem 'Resignation', which inverts the tercets and quatrains. This inversion allows him to oppose childhood and reverie through the evocation of a dreamed and fantasised Orient, to the present time, where the poet must show more moderation.

- Instead of using even-numbered lines such as decasyllables or alexandrines, Verlaine also uses odd-numbered lines. This is particularly the case in 'Cauchemar', where he uses heptasyllables, and in 'Marine' and 'Soleils couchants' where he uses pentasyllables. This is a clear break with classical prosody and the reign of the alexandrine. The odd verse is less regular, breaking the automatism of the reading and thus allowing the reader to have a more personal cadence.

- Verlaine frees himself from the rule of alternating masculine and feminine rhymes. He uses assonance as a discreet musicality and adds interior rhymes, thus giving sound a central place.

- Although Verlaine has a sense of formal perfection and proposes a linear and symbolic poetic form, it is nonetheless close to prose, with texts made to be recited in public expressively. The verse sometimes absorbs turns of oral language and thus reveals an inner song. This is particularly the case in the poem "Sunsets".

THE MAIN THEMES OF THE COLLECTION

The three main themes of the collection are melancholy, time and love, a love that is both idealised and lost.

Melancholy in Verlaine

Melancholy is the central theme. It runs through the whole collection. For Verlaine, it is much more than a feeling. In the 'Melancholia' section, Verlaine seems to take up the theme of Baudelaire's spleen, particularly in the poem 'L'Angoisse', where negation is very present as if the poet was being dragged into nothingness. However, he offers a very personal and intimate writing of the spleen. The memories evoked are vague, which gives them a universal dimension. More than a feeling, melancholy is also a space and a temporality.

It is anchored in landscapes that accentuate this feeling, notably in the poems 'Sunsets' and 'Sentimental Walk'. It refers to the autumn season through the poem « Chanson d'automne » and « Crépuscule du soir mystique ». Verlaine shows himself to be extremely sensitive to a nature that echoes his personal feelings. Thus he writes lyrical poetry, in which musicality plays an important role. The music, present throughout the work, accompanies the melancholy, gives rhythm to the slowness and languor. It is based in particular on the violin, the instrument of sorrow par excellence. Thus, in « Chanson d'automne »:

> *"Violins*
>
> *From autumn*
>
> *Hurt my heart*
>
> *Of a languor*
>
> *Monotonous." (v.2-6)*

Similarly in 'Initium': 'The violins mingled their laughter with the singing of the flutes' (v. 1).

Saturn and the Figure of Time

The theme of time is also present, notably through the figure of Saturn. Saturn is one of the most ancient gods of Lazio and central Italy. An agricultural deity par excellence; he was responsible for protecting the seeds entrusted to the earth. The month of December, when the work of germination began, the prelude to the harvest was dedicated to Saturn. The legend that grew up around him blends Latin and Greek traditions, assimilating him to the figure of Kronos, god of the Hellenes and primordial deity of time. Saturn was predicted to be dethroned by his sons. To escape his fate, he decides to devour them.

His wife, Rhea, horrified by his cruelty, hides the last-born, Jupiter, who drives him out of Olympus. Saturn then leaves Greece for Italy and settles on the right bank of the Tiber, where Rome will be built. He was welcomed by Janus, king of the country, to whom he taught agriculture. In exchange, Janus gave him the hill on the right bank of the Tiber: the Capitol. Often represented with a sickle or a scythe, Saturn suddenly disappears. In his honour, Janus erected an altar and celebrated the Saturnalia festival.

This god, who presides over the period preceding the winter solstice, gives his name to the planet of the solar system, known for its yellow colour and its stellate rings. Since ancient times, it has been famous for its negative influence on human life. It predestines those born under its sign to misfortune, placing them under the sign of time and fatality to which the myth of Saturn refers. Thus, Verlaine takes up an ancient tradition, allowing him to associate melancholy and artistic creation.

In the collection, we find themes reminiscent of this myth, such as the betrayal of women, the impossibility of escaping one's destiny, and the importance of nature and what it offers to men. The question of time is also very present. The 'Prologue' already has a three-part structure: 'In those fabulous times' (v. 1), 'Later' (v. 37) and 'Today' (v. 51), as if Verlaine were undertaking a journey through time. The poem 'Nevermore', which follows the four parts, also refers to the inevitability of time passing. It contains the lexical field of old age: 'old' (v. 1, v. 5), 'old man' (v. 8), 'wrinkles' (v. 9), and 'yellowed' (v. 10). Verlaine shows how time marks both the world and the body. Its force is such that it can neither be slowed down nor prevented from leading slowly towards a foretold destruction.

The third major theme of the collection: love

Love in Verlaine refers to an ideal, but impossible or unhappy love. It is often idealised and disembodied, as in 'Mon rêve familier', where it is about an 'unknown woman' (v. 2), or in 'À une femme', where Verlaine again speaks of a dreamed, imagined woman. When it is not imagined, love is relegated to the distant past, as in 'Vœu' or 'Nevermore'. Otherwise, it can be combined with loneliness and absence, as in 'Promenade sentimentale', where the poet is alone and sad, rehearsing his grief.

The love mentioned in this collection is the love for sensual and dangerous, inaccessible and devious women like those present in «Femme et chatte» or «la chanson des ingénues». In Verlaine's eyes, women are largely responsible for the failure of love and the betrayal that follows. He makes the love of woman an uninterrupted evil. He generalises the feeling and experiences of love intoxicating everyone. He feels guilty for deploring futile loves and for constantly seeking to reinvent others. In this way, Verlaine comes close to a Baudelairian conception of love. He transfigures love relationships in a constant tension between pleasure and sadness, but also between reality and imagination.

This concept of love is of course related to the author's biography and his love partners. At that time, the love of her life was her cousin Elisa, whom her mother had adopted. Rejecting her love, she married a sugarman before dying in childbirth. Verlaine then fell in love with Mathilde Mauté, who was ten years younger than him. He had a child with her, lost interest in her and had many adventures, until his passionate encounter with Arthur Rimbaud.

VERLAINE: SYMBOLIST POET

In contributing to the renewal of poetic expression, Verlaine proposes a work that sublimates the perception of the universe. Like Baudelaire, who paved the way for symbolism with *Les Fleurs du mal*, Verlaine transcribed visions and inner landscapes that represent ideas to which they are linked by analogy. He worked on the art of suggestion, evoking things without naming them simply through the sensations they aroused in him.

The great themes of the *Poèmes saturniens* refer us directly to the great principles of symbolism. Invested with a sacred mission, Verlaine seems to want to show correspondences between the sensible world and the spiritual, invisible and ideal world. He evokes his states of mind through ideal landscapes with hidden realities. He endeavours to describe the flight of time and the vertigo of the moment. Thus, he refuses both rationalism and materialism, seeking to re-discover the mysteries of the world. He describes his dreams and gives full scope to ambivalence and nuance, favouring transience over permanence. He uses symbolic and musical language, translating the fragility of sensations. He favours the liberalisation of verse.

The Poèmes saturniens thus heralded to some extent the emergence of the Symbolist movement, a movement whose codes he would use in his later works such as *Art poétique* (1874), the collection *Jadis et Naguère* (1884) and *Les poètes maudits* (1888). Nevertheless, although Verlaine is sometimes seen as the leader of the Symbolists, he never claimed to be one, preferring to maintain the myth of the cursed poet suffering and dying from physical and social failure.

AVENUES FOR REFLECTION

A FEW QUESTIONS FOR FURTHER REFLECTION...

- In the light of the prologue, what is the place of the poet according to Verlaine?

- In what way can we say that the *Poèmes saturniens* are influenced by Parnassianism?

- Is lead poisoning just melancholy?

- Compare Baudelaire's spleen with Verlaine's melancholy.

- What impression is given by the inversion of quatrains and tercets in the poem 'Resignation'?

- How does the use of odd-numbered lines provide musicality?

- Analyse the importance of sound effects: how do they contribute to the meaning of the poems?

- What is Verlaine's link between literature and the arts?

TO GO FURTHER

REFERENCE EDITION

VERLAINE P., *Poèmes Saturniens*, Gallimard, coll. "Folio", 2018.

BENCHMARK STUDIES

AGUETTANT L., *Verlaine*, Les introuvables, 1978, 240 p.

BERNARDET B. (ed.), *Verlaine, première manière. Poèmes saturniens, Fêtes galantes, Romances sans paroles (1866-1874)*, PUF, coll. "Cned-PUF", 2007.

BORNECQUE J-H., *Les poèmes saturniens de Verlaine*, Nizet, 1967, 255 p.

DUBOIS C., *Étude sur Paul Verlaine: Poèmes saturniens*, Paris, Ellipses, 1998, 96 p.

GUYAUX A. (dir.), *Les premiers recueils de Verlaine. Poèmes saturniens, Fêtes galantes, Romances sans paroles*, Paris, PUPS, 2008, 217 p.

MURPHY S., *Lectures de Verlaine: poèmes saturniens, fêtes galantes, romances sans paroles*, Presses universitaires de Rennes, 2007, 314 p.

MAIN MUSICAL ADAPTATIONS

ABBIATE L., Chanson d'automne, *Pièces pour chant et piano n° 2*, Paris, 1899.

AMIET P., Nevermore, *Four melodies for song and piano*, Paris, 1926.

ANDRÉ J., Chanson d'automne, *Mélodies et chansons n° 2*, Paris, 1928.

ARHAM M., Chanson d'automne, *Douze mélodies, 3e série n° 5*, Paris, 1914.

BELLIARD M., Chanson d'automne, *Quatre mélodies n° 2*, Paris, 1920.

BERNAERT A., Chanson d'automne, *op. 1 n° 1, 3 Mélodies n° 1*, Liège, 1920.

BONNAUD F-L, *Paysages tristes*, Paris, 1897.

BONNEAU P., Nevermore, *SEMI*, Paris, 1955

BORDES C., *Paysages tristes, n° 2*, Paris, 1902.

BRITTEN B., Chanson d'automne, *Quatre chansons françaises No. 4*, London, 1982.

CARPENTER J-A., *Four poems by Paul Verlaine, No. 2*, New York, 1912.

CHARPENTIER G., Chanson d'automne, *Poèmes chantés, n° 14*, Paris, 1894.

DELIUS F., Autumn Song, *Fünf Gesänge, No. 5, Köln am Rhein*, 1915.

De FAY R., Chanson d'automne, *Mélodie n° 2*, Paris, 1902.

FERRE L., Mon rêve familier, Soleils couchants and Chanson d'automne, 1970.

FRAGGI H., Chanson d'automne, *Poèmes en musique, n° 2*, Marseille, 1920.

LIMA FRAGOSO A., *Cinq mélodies de Paul Verlaine, n° 3*, Paris 1917.

FRONTIN G-L., Chanson d'automne, *Sous les chênes verts, n° 7*, Paris, 1912.

HAHN R., Chanson d'automne, *Chansons grises*, n° 1, Paris, 1893.

DE HARTMANN, *Paysages tristes*, No. 5, Paris, 1941.

JOSTEN W., *Trois mélodies de Paul Verlaine*, No. 2, Paris, 1931.

KOVALEV P I., *Six songs on poems by Paul Verlaine*, No. 3, Moscow, 1925.

PANIZZAH, *Nine poems by Paul Verlaine*, no. 1, Milan, 1899.

PASSANI E-B, *Trois poèmes de Verlaine*, n°1, Paris, 1952.

www.brightsummaries.com

Ebook EAN: 9782808686501
Paperback EAN: 9782808697903
Legal Deposit: D/2023/12603/1070

Cover: © Primento
Digital conception by Primento, the digital partner of publishers.